Turning Children into (

Magical Treehouse W(

CW00797070

The stories and characters in this book were **created by children** in a Magical Treehouse Workshop **with a real author & illustrator.** We turned up for the day, inspired the children's imaginations and took their magical creations away to be printed in this very book!

We want you to be next, so contact us today!

Email: info@magicaltreehouse.com
Tel: 07841 635 423 (Todd - Author)

www.MagicalTreehouse.com/workshops

Turning Children into Creators...
Magical Treehouse Workshops

Index

www.MagicalTreehouse.com/workshops

Jolly Jag & Polly Parrot

Created by Kingfisher Class (Y2)

One day Polly Parrot was looking for a mixture of seeds and insects on the rainforest floor for a scrumptious meal. Polly wasn't a very happy parrot, but there was one thing she was excellent at, and that was foraging for food. She always knew how to find the tastiest seeds and juiciest insects to fill her belly.

On this particular day, Polly was just about to gobble up the loveliest insect when she heard a noise coming from behind a nearby bush. "Who is singing that song?" she thought to herself while squinting at the bush to take a closer look.

There, stood behind the bush singing to himself was the most beautifully coloured jaguar. "Hello!" he said in a very joyful fashion while jumping out of the bush and performing a tap dance routine he'd learned from his Mum.

"Leave me alone," says Polly Parrot in her usual miserable fashion. "Oh, don't be like that. My name is Jolly Jag and I think we might be able to help each other," Jolly Jag says with a toothy grin.

Polly Parrot is quite cautious of a jaguar with such large teeth, but she's intrigued by just how jolly Jolly Jag is. "You see Polly," Jolly Jag continues, "I'm not very good at getting food, but I am very good at being happy. When I was watching you back there, it seems you're the total opposite! You can gather food, but you're not exactly...jolly. No offence."

"None taken," Polly says with a grump. "Anyway, it's easy. I guess you don't eat insects and seeds, but you just have to forage around and collect anything that looks yummy. Also, you need to stop singing and dancing. You'll never catch anything with all that noise!"

Before long, Polly Parrot had Jolly Jag dropping down onto his belly and creeping across the rainforest floor as if hunting for food. "See, it's easy Jolly Jag. I told you so," says Polly with a smug grin knowing she has helped Jolly Jag learn how to catch his food, although he still needs to camouflage himself to cover up those gaudy colours!

By the time Polly Parrot opened her eyes, Jolly Jag had gone. "Jolly, where are you?" Polly asks in a confused manner. A minute passed by and it was silent all around.

Polly was just about to start flapping her wings to head back to the safety of the canopy above, when she let out a mighty, "SQUAAAAAWK!" and everything went black. It was Jolly Jag. He'd been practising his new hunting techniques and it worked so well, Polly Parrot had no idea until Jolly Jag was on top of her!

Polly Parrot was annoyed at first, but for the first time in a long time, she started to giggle. The giggle turned into a chuckle and within a few seconds they were both rolling around on the floor laughing out loud. When they finally caught their breath, something magical had happened!

Amidst the laughter, Jolly Jag had passed on his beautiful colours and happiness to Polly Parrot, meaning they had both given something to one another. Polly flew off to the top of the trees the envy of all parrots with her incredible feathers and Jolly Jag was able to hide and catch his meals all on his own without singing or dazzling them with his coat.

From that day forth, Polly Parrot would bring her friends to meet Jolly Jag and they would learn his latest dance moves. Spirits were high in the rainforest as they spent the rest of their lives dancing with very full and round tummies.

MAGICAL TREEHOUSE
WORD & ART IN CAHOOTS!

Turning Children into Creators...
Magical Treehouse Workshops

Created by...

Otter Class (Y1)

Zebra & Croc

There was once a crocodile who could not come out in the sunshine and had to stay underwater all day long, because his skin was too sensitive to the sun's rays! The only thing you would ever see of this rather odd croc during the day was his little nostrils poking out above the water so that he could breathe!

As meals for crocodiles tend to come along during the day, this meant he was very, very hungry as you can imagine. What a sorry state of affairs.

Waiting under the water one fine day ready to strike for a meal, he saw ripples coming from the surface. Now was his chance to pounce, grab himself a juicy meal and get back under the water before the sun could cause him any harm.

"1, 2, 3..." Croc said to himself and leaped towards the rippling water! Sadly, before he knew it he was snapping fresh air with a harem of zebra's howling with laughter on the water's edge. He just didn't have the energy to move fast enough.

"What are you doing, Croc?" asked Zebra from the front of the harem. "I was trying to gobble you up, but I haven't eaten for a long time and I simply couldn't move fast enough," Croc replied.

Once Zebra and her friends had stopped laughing and dancing around Croc in the water to show they were too fast for him, they came up with an idea.

"How about we help each other?" Zebra said. "If you let us bath in this water and drink whenever we need to, we'll help shepherd fish in your direction so you can have a tasty meal."

Croc couldn't believe his luck! Not only did he have a simple way to get a full meal without leaving the water, he had a whole harem of friends he could enjoy his days with.

True to their word, the zebra's would form a 'v' shape whenever they visited the water and our beloved crocodile would sit there rather gleefully as the zebra's pushed all the nearby fish into his wide open mouth.

"We're a great team, even if you are a little noisy," Croc thought to himself surrounded by zebras swimming, bathing and lolloping in the water.

Turning Children into Creators...
Magical Treehouse Workshops

Created by...

Hedgehog Class (Y1)

www.MagicalTreehouse.com/workshops

Giraffe & Hippo

Hippo lived in her idea of heaven. There was enough water for her to swim and bathe in, while surrounded by the most beautiful fish. Hippo enjoyed nothing better than simply watching her watery world pass by.

Unfortunately for Hippo, the water level around her was dropping every year due to the amount of animals that were now drinking from her rather large pond. Even the annual rains couldn't top it up and her rain dances just weren't working.

The water was getting so low, Hippo knew she had to act! Before long, she saw a tower of giraffes approaching the water preparing themselves for a drink. Giraffes, as we all know, are rather large creatures and they drink a lot of water!

Hippo dropped down below the water and waited for the right moment. As she saw a huge black tipped tongue reach down to scoop up a bucket load of water, she reached up and pinched it between her feet!

"YEEEEEEEEEEOOOOOW!" cried Giraffe, "What did you do that for?" he asked with a tear in his eye.

"I'm sick of all the animals coming from far and wide to come and drink my water!" screamed Hippo with an angry face. "I love my home and it's being destroyed by all these thirsty tongues!"

"It's not your water," said Giraffe rather bravely. "We need somewhere to drink after all. We have calves to keep healthy and there's nowhere else to drink for miles around."

Hippo had listened to Giraffe and realised she was being rather selfish, then suddenly an idea popped in her head. "I've got it," she cried and began to wander off away from her water.

Just as Giraffe was about to ask where she was going, Hippo started digging a hole. "Don't just stand there," she said. "The rains will be coming soon and we need somewhere else for you all to drink."

Smiling, the giraffes galloped over and soon every animal around was helping Hippo dig, dig and dig some more. Before long, they had a dug a hole big enough for everyone to drink from.

Hippo looked up at Giraffe and said, "Now you can drink from both holes and there will be enough for everyone. You can drink to your hearts content and I can swim in two different pools. Just make sure you always come back and say hello."

Giraffe smiled and said, "Of course we will." Then the sky crackled and rain came down heavier than it had for many years. It seems a mixture of teamwork and Hippo's rain dances had finally saved her home while keeping all the nearby animal's thirst quenched for years and years to come.

Created by...

Owl Class (Y2)

Ruby Red Riding Hood

A long time ago there lived a young gorilla called Ruby Red Riding Hood.

One day, Ruby Red Riding Hood's mum asked her to take some cakes to her granny who was ill. So she put on her cloak, packed up a basket and skipped off through the woods to granny's house.

Ruby Red Riding Hood hadn't gone far when she met a pirate with a wooden leg and a hook instead of a hand.

He asked her where she was going. "I'm going to take these cakes to my grandma's house."

"That's very kind of you, but be careful," warned the pirate, "there's a sinister snake in these woods and he's always hungry."

Ruby Red Riding Hood bravely skipped on a bit faster. Behind a tree the sinister snake watched her. He was feeling rather hungry. He would have liked to have swallowed Ruby Red Riding Hood whole there and then, but he could hear the pirate nearby, so he thought better of it.

Instead, he thought of a clever plan, and slithered off in the direction of grandma's house. When the snake got to granny's house he rudely let himself in and greedily swallowed up granny in one gulp. Then, he squeezed his fat body into granny's night-gown put on her night-cap and glasses and lay in her bed.

A short time later, Ruby Red Riding Hood arrived at granny's house. Granny didn't look like herself at all. "What big eyes you have," said Ruby Red Riding Hood. " All the better to see you with my dear," said the snake.

"But what a big tongue you have!" "All the better to taste...I mean smell you with my dear," said the snake.

"Granny, what big fangs you have!" "All the better to eat you with!" said the snake with a wicked hiss. He raised to strike from the bed and began to chase a very frightened Ruby Red Riding Hood. She screamed very loudly!

Luckily, the pirate heard the noise and just as the snake was about to eat up the delicious Ruby Red Riding Hood, he burst in the door and stamped on the snake's belly with his wooden leg, forcing granny's head up and out of the snake's mouth!

Ruby Red Riding Hood, granny and the pirate all sat down to tea and cakes and they lived happily ever after. Especially granny, who loved her fantastic new snake skin suit!

Turning Children into Creators...
Magical Treehouse Workshops

Created by...

Nursery

Jack & The Beanstalk

Once upon a time there was a boy called Jack who lived with his mother. They were very poor and all they had was a pig.

One morning, Jack's mother told Jack to take their pig to market and sell her. On the way, Jack met a man wearing a rather interesting suit.

He gave Jack some magic beans for the pig. Jack took the beans and went back home. When Jack's mother saw the beans she was so angry, turned bright and almost popped! She threw the beans out of the window in a fit of rage and sent Jack to bed.

The next morning, Jack looked out of the window and there stood a giant beanstalk. He went outside and started to climb the beanstalk, right up to the sky and through the clouds where Jack saw a beautiful castle.

He went inside in the castle and soon heard a voice, "Fee, Fi, Fo, Fum!" Jack ran into a cupboard to hide.

An enormous giant came into the room and sat down. On the table there was a hen and a golden harp.

"Lay!" said the giant. The hen laid an egg made of solid gold.

"Sing!" said the giant and the harp began to sing. Soon the giant was asleep and Jack jumped out of the cupboard.

He took the hen and the harp, but all of a sudden noticed something he liked much more...the giant's hairy toe! Jack grabbed his toe, which popped off in his hand and he made a dash for the door.

Suddenly, the harp sang, "Master, master, that boy has your hairy toe!" The giant woke up with all the kerfuffle and boomed in a confused manner, "Fee, Fum, Fi, Fo...**where's my hairy toe?**"

Jack ran and started climbing down the beanstalk. The giant came down after him, shouting even louder, "Fee, Fum, Fi, Fo...**who's got my hairy toe?**"

Jack shouted, "Mother, help!" Jack's mother took an axe and chopped down the beanstalk. The giant fell and crashed to the ground, but within a second or two he got back up!

Jack and his mother stood in front of the giant and there was no toe to be seen. The giant was now looking over the heads of Jack and his mother...

"You've got my hairy toe!"

MAGICAL TREEHOUSE
WORD & ART IN CAHOOTS!

Turning Children into Creators...
Magical Treehouse Workshops

Created by...

Fox & Squirrel Classes
(Reception)

The Humongous Treasure Chest!

Once upon a time, there was a pirate that gathered so much loot, he decided to bury chests full of treasure across the land.

The only problem was, he couldn't remember which chest had what treasure in. Once he found the exact spot on his map, he started to dig and soon came across a humongous treasure chest.

The pirate hooked the humongous treasure chest and pulled with all his might, but it would not budge! He shouted to Bunny, who was eating carrots in the same field, to give him some help.

Then, together, they pulled and pulled and pulled and pulled, but the humongous treasure chest still would not budge!

So the pirate and Bunny called for Giraffe who was munching away at the leaves of a nearby tree. Giraffe galloped over ready to help.

All together, they pulled and pulled and pulled and pulled, but the humongous treasure chest still would not budge!

So, the pirate, Bunny and Giraffe shouted to Gorilla who going to see his grandmother. Gorilla mooched over to help.

All together, they pulled, and pulled and pulled and pulled, but the humongous treasure chest still would not budge!

So, the pirate, Bunny, Giraffe and Gorilla shouted to Zebra, who whinnied and galloped over to lend a helping hoof.

All together, they pulled, and pulled and pulled and pulled, but the humongous treasure chest still would not budge!

So, the pirate, Bunny, Giraffe, Gorilla and Zebra called Snake who slithered over and wrapped around Zebra's leg ready to help.

All together, they pulled, and pulled and pulled and pulled, but the humongous treasure chest still would not budge!

So, the pirate, Bunny, Giraffe, Gorilla, Zebra and Snake beckoned the chicken that lays golden eggs. She clucked and was soon ready to help.

All together, they pulled, and pulled and pulled and pulled and suddenly…

"CRASH, BANG, WALLOP!"

Out of the ground came a humongous treasure chest full of 24 carat gold in the shape of carrots! The pirate was very pleased and gave everyone some of the loot for their hard work.

Everyone thanked the pirate, apart from the chicken who simply said, "It's OK I have enough gold as I lay golden eggs!"

Turning Children into Creators...
Magical Treehouse Workshops

Thank you Clover Hill Infant & Nursery!

We want you to be next, so contact us today!

Email: info@magicaltreehouse.com

Tel: 07841 635 423 (Todd - Author)

www.**MagicalTreehouse**.com/workshops

For workshops & books by Todd & James, please visit...
www.MagicalTreehouse.com

The Dragon's Disguise - Vol.1

The Dragon's Disguise - Vol.2

The Dragon's Disguise - Vol.3

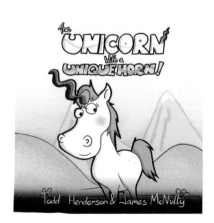

The Unicorn with a Unique Horn!

The Boggle Eyed Gog

Ugly Pugly & Pigly Winks

 Magical Treehouse

 @MagicalTreehous

Printed in Great Britain
by Amazon